WITHDRAWN

D0572893

The Boy Who Wouldn't Swim

by
Deb Lucke

CLARION BOOKS ✷ NEW YORK

Clarion Books
a Houghton Mifflin Company imprint
215 Park Avenue South,
New York, NY 10003
Copyright © 2008 by Deb Lucke

The illustrations were executed in gouache.
The text was set in 15-point Addled.

All rights reserved.

For information about permission to
reproduce selections from this book,
write to Permissions, Houghton Mifflin
Company, 215 Park Avenue South,
New York, NY 10003.

www.clarionbooks.com

Manufactured in China

Library of Congress Cataloging-in-Publication Data
Lucke, Deb. The Boy who wouldn't swim / by Deb Lucke.
p. cm.
Summary: One very hot summer, Eric Dooley
watches his younger sister go from her first
swimming lesson all the way to the diving
board, while his fear of the water
keeps him from joining her and
the rest of the people of
Clermont County in the pool.
ISBN 978-0-618-91484-5
[1. Swimming—Fiction.
2. Swimming pools—Fiction.
3. Fear—Fiction. 4. Brothers and
sisters—Fiction.]
I. Title. II. Title: Boy
who would not swim.

PZ7.L9717Boy 2008
[E]—dc22

2007022120

WKT 10 9 8 7 6 5 4 3 2 1

For Eric

It was so hot that summer that the whole town practically lived in the pool. The Wilsons, the Hurlbuts, the Ignazios, the Wittemeirs, and the Dooleys were there so much, you'd think

they got out of the water only to sleep. There wasn't a person in Clermont County who didn't have prune toes.

Except Eric Dooley.

Nothing would get Eric into the pool. When his mom came over wearing her swim cap and an encouraging smile, he said, **"No!"** before she could even open her mouth.

He said the same thing when one of the Wilson twins invited him to an underwater tea party. And when Mr. Ignazio threw a nickel into the pool and yelled, **"Finders keepers!"**

He was so
busy ignoring
them that at first
he didn't notice his
younger sister, Jessica,
getting the swim lesson
meant for him! "Put your
face in the water and blow
bubbles, dear," his mom said.
"*Bluubbbb, bluuuubbbb, bluuubb.*"
Eric didn't know which was
worse, being afraid to
learn how to swim
or being jealous
of Jess learning
how to swim.

His mom saw him watching.
"Want to join us, Eric?"
"Are you kidding?
She just blew **spit** all
over the pool!" he shouted.

10

Rex, the lifeguard, pointed a warning finger at Jess and blew his whistle. "Pool rules: No Spitting," he said.

A remarkably short while later, his mom said,
"Look, Jessica's dog-paddling. You could too, Eric."
Eric closed his eyes and feigned indifference.
He kept them shut so long, his eyelids tanned.

When he finally opened them, it was the end of June.
Jessica was swimming right across the middle of the
pool, where the water was the deepest!
She looked really pleased with herself, too.

Under his thick coating of sunblock, Eric was green with envy. He stood up and yelled, "**Shark!**"

Jessica panicked. She dog-paddled, breaststroked, and crawled until she reached the solid ground of Mr. Ignazio's head. Rex, the lifeguard, had to climb down from his chair to pry her off. She took the last few strands of Mr. Ignazio's hair with her.

Then his mom gave Eric a time out.
By the time it was over, Jessica had learned
how to swim underwater! He couldn't believe it.
All he'd learned how to do was freckle.

When Jess came up for a breath,
Eric yelled, "**Baby pee!**"

Jess screamed and scrambled up the ladder.
Right behind her were Mrs. Wittemeir, all the
Hurlbuts, and the Wilsons. Mr. Ignazio got out,
too, being careful to keep his distance from
Jess. The rest of the Dooleys got out as well,

although they suspected that Eric was making it up.
Especially since all the babies were over in the baby pool.
   Rex had to test the water and prove it was clean while
the whole town looked on—hot, sweaty, and irritated,
just the way Eric had been all summer.

After that, Eric had a long time out. A very, very long time out. When he was finally back in his lounge chair, it was mid-July. He was shocked to see Jessica on the end of the diving board. Their eyes locked and she said,

"Naa, na, naa, na, naa, naa."

Then she jumped off!

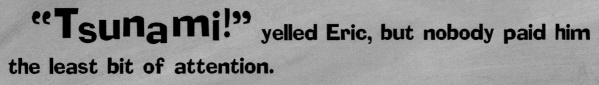

"**Tsunami!**" yelled Eric, but nobody paid him the least bit of attention.

Eric sat in his chair on the hot concrete and steamed for most of August while Jess jumped off the diving board again and again.

Eric was so hot, he thought he might melt.
But the idea of plunging into that bottomless
pit of icy blue water made him sweat even more.
 Finally, he couldn't stand it any longer. When no
one was looking, he snuck over to the baby pool
and waded in. Instantly, he was nice and cool.
At least, from the ankles down.

But the babies were giving him weird looks. They began to cry.
Then wail. Eric realized they were right. He was no baby!

He got out, went to the big pool, and, without thinking about it *too* much, took a deep breath and climbed down the ladder. He made it as far as the second rung.

Pool Edge

Eventually, he let his mom pry
his hands off the ladder and
tow him around.

26

It was so nice and cool in the water that sometimes, just once in a while, he forgot to be scared.

The next day he got his first swim lesson. Without his giraffe!

Before long, he had prune toes, like everyone else.

And just like that he went from being the boy
who wouldn't swim to being the boy who wouldn't
get out of the pool. By the last week of August,
Eric could dog-paddle, breaststroke, and crawl.

He had an underwater tea party with Jess and the Wilson twins. He was thinking about giving the diving board a try . . .

. . . when the pool closed for the season. The Wilsons, the Hurlbuts, the Ignazios, and the Wittemeirs packed up their sunblock and damp towels and went home. The Dooleys would've done the same, but Eric wouldn't get out of the water. Rex, the lifeguard, needed to leave for college, but he couldn't go off-duty as long as anyone was in the pool.

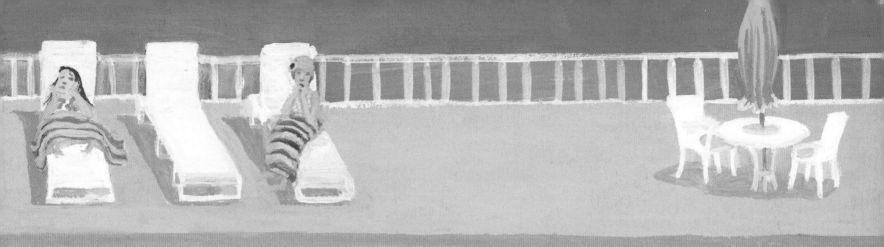

Nothing would get Eric out. Not even after the weather turned. The Dooley family sat on their lounge chairs—cold, shivering, and irritated—while Eric swam back and forth across the pool.

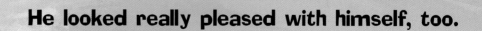

He looked really pleased with himself, too.

CONTRA COSTA COUNTY LIBRARY